THIS BOOK
BELONGS TO:

....

To my darling grandsons, AJ and Matthew.
Love, your Nana

www.mascotbooks.com

No, No, No Nuts for Me

For more information, please contact:
Mascot Books
560 Herndon Parkway #120
Herndon, VA 20170
info@mascotbooks.com

Library of Congress Control Number: 2016914976

CPSIA Code: PRT1116A
ISBN-13: 978-1-63177-977-0

Printed in the United States

NO, NO, NO NUTS FOR ME

Written and Illustrated by
Carol Florio

My name is Teddy Bear.
I live with

my Mama Bear,
Daddy Bear,

and
Baby Brother
Bear.

This is our house.

One day we went on a
picnic and I ate a nut...

I got very, very sick.

NO, NO, NO!
My eyes got puffy...
my mouth got puffy...
my body was very, very red and itchy!

Sooo...

I went to the doctor
and the doctor said,
"Teddy Bear,
NO NUTS, **NO, NO.**
Because you have a nut allergy."

Mama and Daddy Bear said

"NO NUTS,

NO, NO."

NO NUTS for me,
NO, NO
'cause I have a nut allergy.

No peanuts...
no tree nuts,

NO, NO.

No nuts in my food.
No nuts in my sweets.
NO nuts in anything.

NO, NO, NO.

No nuts in my house,
   no nuts at my school.

No eating nuts.

NO, NO.

NO NUTS

with my friends.

No nuts outside.

No nuts inside.

No eating
nuts anywhere.

NO, NO, NO!

NO, NO,

NO NUTS FOR ME.

Sooo...

now I eat EVERYTHING nut-free
because I have an allergy.

Now for my Nana Bear's No Nutter Cookies.

YUM, YUM, YUM!

NO NUTTER COOKIES

Directions

1. In a large bowl, mix together flour, baking powder, and salt.

2. In processor, cream butter. Gradually add sugar and beat until fluffy. Add egg yolk and extract until well blended.

3. Add flour mixture gradually—mix well.

4. Wrap the dough in wax paper and refrigerate for ½ hour.

5. Pre-heat oven to 350 degrees Fahrenheit.

6. Put dough into a cookie press OR drop teaspoons of dough onto cold cookie sheets.

7. Leave plain or decorate with sprinkles.

8. Bake 8-10 minutes or until edges are golden brown.

9. Cool and ENJOY!

Ingredients

- 2 cups flour
- 1 cup butter
- 1 egg yolk
- 1 tsp baking powder
- ⅛ tsp salt
- ¾ cup sugar
- 1 tsp vanilla extract OR
  1 tsp lemon extract

SO SCRUMPTIOUS!

Information on Peanut and Tree Nut Allergies

- Nut allergies in children have tripled since 1997 and only 20% will outgrow this allergy.
- Siblings of allergic children are at an increased risk for nut allergies.
- Peanuts grow underground and are part of the legume family. All other nuts grow on trees. Tree nuts include: almonds, brazil nuts, cashews, filberts, hazelnuts, hickory nuts, macadamia nuts, pecans, pine nuts, pistachios, and walnuts.
- Peanuts and tree nuts are not the same. If allergic to one, you may need to avoid the other (25-40% of children are allergic to both). Get allergy testing and your allergist will advise you.
- Even trace amounts of a nut, whether swallowed or inhaled, can cause an allergic reaction. This can range from a mild to a life threatening anaphylactic reaction.
- Exposure to nuts directly (by eating or skin contact), by cross-contact (foods exposed to nuts during processing), or by inhalation (dust, aerosol, or in an enclosed area) can cause allergic symptoms within minutes and can become severe in 10 to 60 minutes. Symptoms range from minor (runny nose, itching, tingling, and a few hives) to major (swelling, multiple hives, dizzy, short of breath, low blood pressure, pale skin, blue lips, and loss of consciousness).

To prevent allergic reaction, it is essential to adhere to strict avoidance of all nuts and nut products:

1. Check labels before you buy or use a product (check prior to every purchase, since companies can change ingredients). Don't ignore a label that states food was processed in a factory that could be contaminated with nut products.
2. Foods that do not contain nuts can get contaminated by being made on the same equipment or shared space as those made with nuts, like in restaurants or ice cream parlors (peanut protein can last up to 100 days). In restaurants, even if you order nut-free, you are still at risk, especially in Asian and Mexican restaurants that use nuts in some of their cooking.
3. Foods that may have hidden nuts are sauces, gravies, extracts, glazes, oils (arachis oil is peanut oil), candy, baked goods, chocolate, ice cream, cereals, soup, honey, grain bread, veggie burgers, and international foods (never assume that a food doesn't contain nuts).
4. Check lotion, shampoo, soap, and pet food for nut additives.

- FALCPA (Food Allergen Labeling and Consumer Protection Act) requires all packaged food sold in the U.S. that contains peanuts to be listed but there is no requirement to list indirect contact with nut sources.

Every family must have an action plan to protect their child

1. Designate EpiPen locations both inside and outside the house (check expiration date regularly).

2. Carry two EpiPens (epinephrine auto-injection) at all times. Practice using it.

3. If a severe reaction happens, use an EpiPen and call 911. If symptoms have not improved after 7-15 minutes, repeat EpiPen. Seek medical attention immediately. Even if symptoms cease, delayed reaction can occur. Get to the emergency room for observation.

4. Your child should wear a med alert bracelet and as they get older be taught to use the EpiPen and not share food.

5. Make sure your child's caregivers—administrators, teachers, relatives, friends, neighbors, drivers, babysitters, and coaches—know about your child's allergy, can recognize symptoms, know where the EpiPen is and how to use it, and to call 911 immediately.

6. Flight precautions include: notifying airline ahead of time to not serve nuts; taking an early flight; wiping seating area; and letting people in seats around you know *no nuts*. Delta and Jet Blue are the airlines most considerate of nut allergies.

Remember: many people don't understand the seriousness of an allergic nut reaction. IT'S UP TO YOU TO PROTECT YOUR CHILD!

ABOUT THE AUTHOR

Carol Florio is a registered nurse and after forty-five years working in hospitals, emergency rooms, schools, and home care, she recently retired. She has taught in vocational schools, worked in the allergy field, and cared for both adult and pediatric patients. She moved from Long Island, New York to Missouri to be near her two young grandsons. Although she has previously published medical articles, this is her first children's book.

TURN THE PAGE
AND FIND A STICKER
JUST FOR YOU!